Johnny McGee
AND HIS SWEET PURPLE PANTS
WRITTEN AND ILLUSTRATED BY
Nikki Cooper

Dream Big, Be Inspired, & Stay Sweet!
Nikki Cooper

LITTLE CREEK PRESS
A DIVISION OF KRISTIN MITCHELL DESIGN, LLC
Mineral Point, Wisconsin USA

Little Creek Press®
A Division of Kristin Mitchell Design, LLC
5341 Sunny Ridge Road
Mineral Point, Wisconsin 53565

Illustrator: Nikki Cooper
Editor: Carrie Stidwell O'Boyle
Book Design and Project Coordination: Little Creek Press

First Edition
July 2014

Text copyright © 2014 Nikki Cooper

Illustrations copyright © 2014 Nikki Cooper

All rights reserved.
No part of this book may be used or reproduced
in any manner whatsoever without written
permission from the author.

Printed in Wisconsin, United States of America.

For more information or to order books:
coopfarm@mhtc.net or www.littlecreekpress.com

Library of Congress Control Number: 2014943135

ISBN-10: 0989978060
ISBN-13: 978-0-9899780-6-4

DEDICATION

To the icing on the cake, the chocolate chips
in the cookie and the sprinkles on top, my family:
BOB, BEN, GRACIE and BRODY,
you are the sweetest, and I wouldn't
be complete without you!

ACKNOWLEDGEMENTS

To all of those who have inspired and encouraged
me along the way, especially my parents,
and to my old pal Jake who
taught me how to draw.

Sneaky Pete is on the hunt for a sweet treat!
Find Sneaky Pete hidden 14 times within the book.

There once was a boy named Johnny McGee,
Who was in a predicament, as you will soon see.
From the top of his head to the heel of his shoe,
Johnny was covered in icky, sticky goo.

What was the source of that great gummy mess?
Well, let's leave that for Johnny to confess.

"I like sugary snacks, they are hard to beat.
A sweet little treat, that's what I eat.
Gumdrops, lollipops, and all the rest,
That's what I like the very best."

Johnny's favorite purple pants were oh so coated in goo.
His parents warned him, "Young man, ants will come after you!"
Ants crave delicious sugar and that is the truth.
Stupendously tremendous is their sweet tooth.

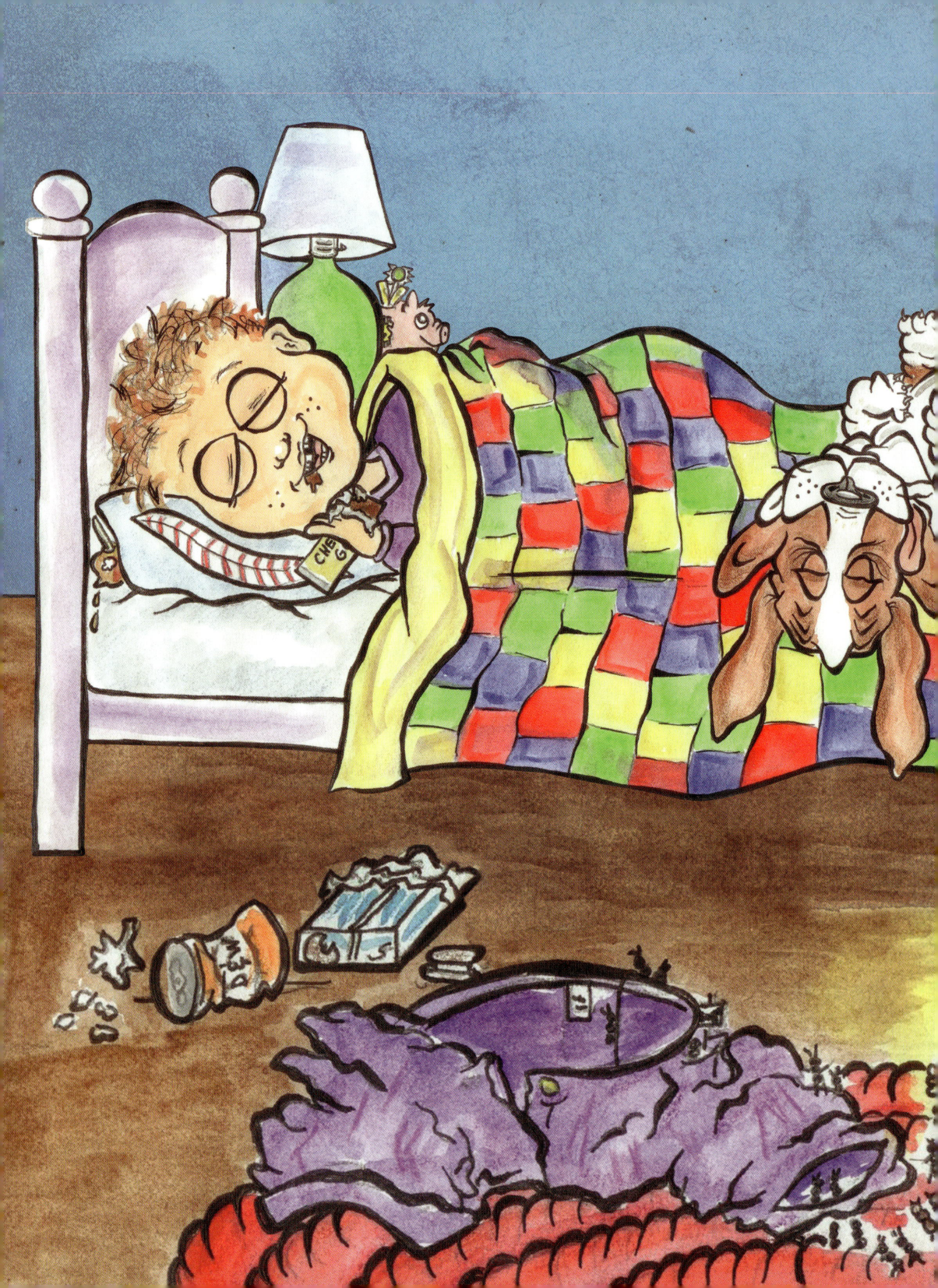

Those pants were a jackpot! It was like striking gold,
They called in their cousins — or so I was told.

The carpenter and the army ants
Lead the trail to the purple pants.

With their ladders, pulleys and tools galore,
They had heard news of candy and were looking for more.

And so it was the very next morning,
Johnny put on his pants, and then without warning...
He began to squiggle and prance,
All because of those sugar-crazed ants!

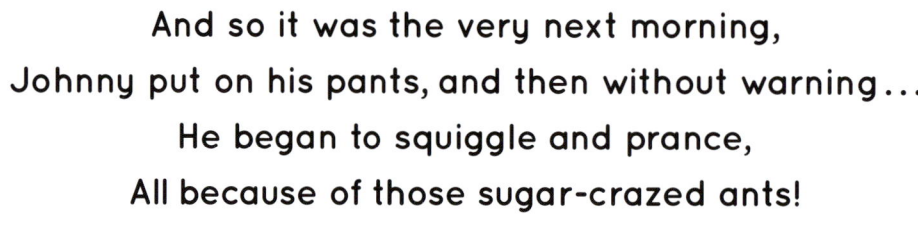

Johnny tickled at breakfast,

At lunch got a twitch,

By supper it hit him a full-blown itch.

By bedtime Johnny was very tired,
Meanwhile, the ants had become increasingly wired.

"We are ants, we are ants,
we are making Johnny dance!"

The next day at school the teacher was shrill.
She scolded young Johnny, "You'd better sit still!"

At recess, Johnny got twisted up in the swing,
The kids laughed and pointed as the ants did their thing.

The school called his parents: "Your son's behavior is outrageous!
Take him to the doctor. He could be contagious!"

The doctor looked at Johnny and scratched his bald head.
"Very interesting case indeed," he said.

A nurse caught a tiny ant wandering by,
"Eureka, Eureka!" she let out a cry.
"Johnny McGee you have ants in your pants!
They are attracted to sugar and are making you dance!
You need to run, you need to play,
Less sugar, young man will keep the ants away…

Go for a swim… ride a bike!
Stop giving those ants just what they like.

Eat broccoli, carrots or even beets.
They are so much healthier than those sugary treats."

Johnny obeyed the doctor's prescription.
He enjoyed exercise and cared about his nutrition.

Finally, one day, all of the sugar ran dry,
And with nothing to nibble, the ants started to cry.

Those sad little ants marched out onto the floor.
They marched out by twos and they marched out by fours.

The moral of the story is this you see,
You might just end up like Johnny McGee.

Constant snacking on chocolate, taffy, and ice cream,
Will make you the target of every ant's dream.

If you munch on all sorts of sugary goo,
You had better watch out, or one day...
Those ants could come after YOU!

"We are ants, we are ants,
we are coming to make you dance!"

ABOUT THE AUTHOR/ILLUSTRATOR

Nikki Cooper lives on a farm in southwest Wisconsin in the little town of Wiota, with her husband, three children and lots of animals. She began drawing cartoons for her local paper at the age of 16 and continued as she attended college. She obtained degrees in animal science and agricultural education from the University of Wisconsin-Platteville. Nikki's love of animals and passion for art has served her well in her current occupation as an artist. She creates comical fabric mache sculptures from recycled materials which she likes to call Nik-er-Doodles. Nikki also enjoys teaching art to children and adults alike. She works out of the Green Chicks Studio in Monroe, Wisconsin.

Contact Nikki:

7310 Hawley Road
Argyle, Wisconsin 53504

coopfarm@mhtc.net
ncooper@greenchicksstudio.com

www.greenchicksstudio.com